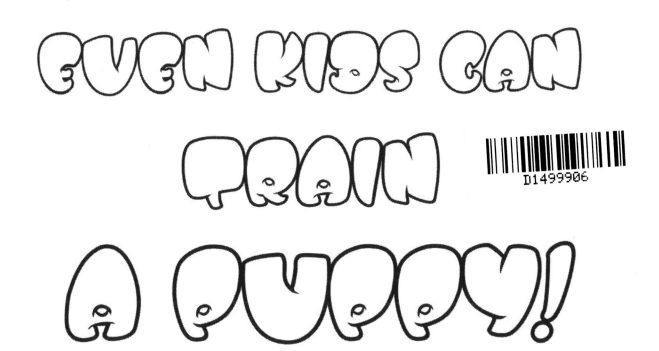

EVEN KIDS CAN TRAIN A PUPPY!

BASIC AND EASY DOG TRAINING
COLORING BOOK FOR KIDS 5 to 12

Joan Toohey

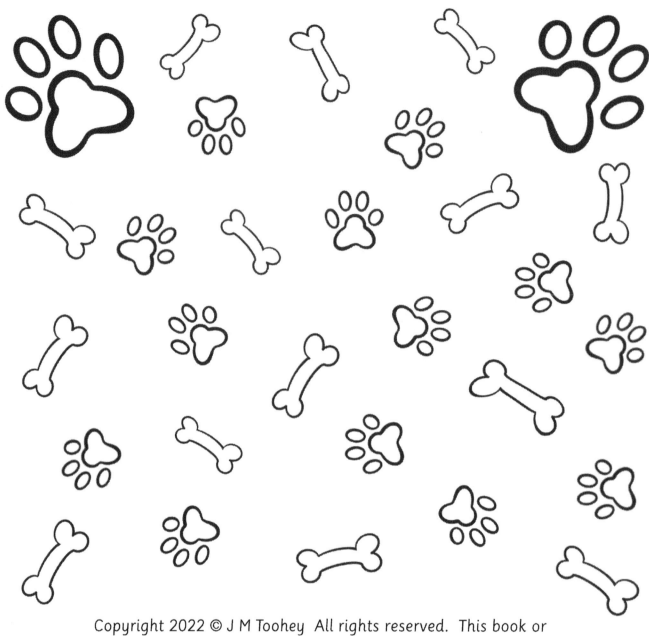

Illustrations, Interior layout, Format, and cover designed by Sunil Nissanka (Top rated freelancer on Upwork.com)
Contact: sumudamar@gmail.com

INTRODUCTION: For the Parents

There are a lot of books and resources out there about how to train a perfect puppy.

Some are loaded with an over-abundance of information which can make one dizzy reading. Not to mention confused as many sources of information contradict each other!

Others share some not very easy and unnecessary training tactics that may frustrate a child... and many busy parents....to the point they give up or don't even want to try to work with their puppy anymore.

This book is going to help you and your child train a HAPPY puppy using a common sense and caring approach. Perfect is not the goal when we first take home our loving and excited puppy.

My experience of over 45 years of training my own puppies with kids at home has taught me that if you have a happy puppy and use simple training techniques, you will likely end up with a happy family dog who is perfect for you. You can always move on to more advanced training systems as your puppy grows.... but perhaps your goal is not to win the Westminster Kennel World Class dog show! If you just want to have a happy, loyal, life-long furry friend, these simple steps are for you!

NOTE: Pronouns can be confusing! I don't like to call my pets "it". I use different versions of pronouns throughout this book when referring to the puppy. He, She, They, Them

TABLE OF CONTENTS

1. FIRST THINGS FIRST-

Before You Bring Your Puppy Home, Understand What You're Getting Into! When you take home a fuzzy, bouncing puppy, your life will never be the same again! Your puppy depends on you to understand his/her basic needs. A happy pet is one who gets not only love and attention, but one who learns to be a well-behaved member of the family! When considering taking a puppy home with you, it is important to remember that it is a lifetime obligation. Your furry friend relies upon you for their safety, health, and happiness. **Make sure you choose a puppy that will be the right size dog for your family when he grows up! And the right size for the home you are making his own.**

2. BASIC NECESSITIES

Here is a list of the things you will want to have on hand to take care of your puppy with a brief description of how it will fit into the daily routine and training.

✓ Food and Water Bowls
   Always keep fresh water available for your puppy 24/7. You want your dog to
   stay hydrated. Make sure your puppy has ready access to his water bowl.

✓ Puppy Food
   Puppies usually eat a special puppy food rich in nutrients to help them grow strong bones and muscle. Sometimes you might have to try a different brand than the one you first choose. It is not unusual. Your vet will help you with choosing the right food for you puppy.

✓ Soft Puppy Bed

✓ Blankets for Crate or Kennel.
Sometimes puppies can get cold at night. A warm and cozy blanket can help to cut down on whining.

✓ Snuggly bedtime toy.
This toy will indicate to your puppy that it is time for bed. Put it with him when you tuck him in for the night. Use this toy only for bedtime.

✓ Correctly Sized Crate/Kennel for your puppy.
Sometimes puppies get bigger that you expected! Depending on your dog's breed, pick a kennel that he will be comfortable in for the first 6 months. If he outgrows it, you will need to get another one.

✓ Toys

Puppies have very sharp teeth! Start out with 4 or 5 toys that he will chew instead of your fingers! You will see what chew toys or bones your puppy likes to play with best.

✓ Right sized collar for your puppy

A Gentle Lead Collar or a No-Pull Harness is usually best to avoid pulling on the leash. Easy on the puppy and easy on you!

✓ ID Tag and if possible, a microchip so if your puppy ever gets lost, you can find him.

✓ A Leash. There are a variety of leashes for dogs on the market. If you decide to use a gentle lead collar or no-pull harness, a soft natural fibers leash is a good choice. But pick the one that works best for your puppy and for you!

✓ Stain and Odor Remover

Accidents happen. Getting to the odor as soon as possible is important. Dogs are drawn to odors and will pee in the same place all the time. Gett the odor out as soon as possible. Arm and Hammer. Pet Rug Powder helps a lot!

✓ Accident Pads

Try not to train you puppy to go potty on accident pads. It is always best to get them outside to do their business. However, there are exceptions. For instance, if you live in a high rise condo in a city, it may be necessary to use an accident pad. If possible, place the pad outside on a balcony deck or patio. He still learns the idea that outside is for going potty.

✓ Grooming supplies: puppy shampoo, puppy comb and brush, towels to dry puppy off, toothbrush and doggy toothpaste.

✓ Puppy Training Treats

It is possible to train your puppy without treats but it is more difficult. Use them sparingly and stop using them once the puppy has learned his command. Positive reinforcement of the command with a Good Dog and a pat will be all you need to continue the good behaviors.

3. Give Your Puppy a Safe and Cozy Home.... puppy proof your home

Make sure you pick up and put out of sight anything you don't want your puppy to chew or break! Shoes, socks, slippers, TV remotes, your toys, electrical and computer wires, throw pillows, small rugs, plants, trash cans, toxins and cleaning supplies! If your house has a fenced in yard, that is perfect. You and your puppy can play freely! But if not, make sure you take your dog out on a leash so he can't run away and get hurt or hit by a car. Maybe you have a dog park nearby so that you can take your puppy there to play with other dogs off-leash. This is a great way to teach your puppy how to get along with others! It is called "socializing your dog".

If you live in the country, remember to protect your pets from predators like coyotes. Especially small puppies!

4. Decide Where Your Puppy is going to sleep.... Set up her bed or kennel

For the first 2 or 3 weeks, you can let your puppy sleep next to your bed in his own bed or crate. Make his crate comfy with blankets and cuddly soft toy. Get that set up before you bring your puppy home so it is ready for him. If you are going to use a crate or kennel, best to put that in your room also. Your puppy may like to go into his kennel during the day to take naps. After 2 or 3 weeks of his bed or kennel in your room, if you don't want him to always sleep there, take his bed to a place that is close by so that he learns that he is still safe. Stay consistent. Your puppy will learn that his bed or kennel is a safe place for him to hang out. As he gets older, you can move the kennel to another area of the home and your dog will be happy to stay there.

5. It's Time to Bring Your Puppy Home!

This is the hardest part for your puppy. When you bring your puppy home, the first day is scary for him. Everything is strange and new. Play with your puppy a lot this first day. Reassure him with pats. Let him get used to his new home and all the fun sniffing he will be doing to learn about his new place in your world.

One of the first things you want to do is bring your puppy to the vet. Your vet will tell you what the best foods are for your puppy. She will also give your puppy the proper vaccinations for protection.... like a rabies shot and a distemper shot. Your vet will put you on the right track toward a healthy dog!

6. It's Time to Plan Your Puppy's Daily Routine!

Everybody knows how much puppies love treats! But the best treat for you is the genuine love, pleasure and joy your puppy will give you every day. This makes up for the work you will have to do to make your puppy the pride and joy of your life! To guarantee your puppy's and your own happiness, this book will teach you tips and tricks to use to be a responsible and dependable pet parent!

7. It's time to eat!

It's time to feed your puppy! Dogs need the right kind of food for them. Not people food. There are lots of quality puppy and dog foods available. Little dogs don't eat the same food as big dogs. Puppies have a special diet for their first year while they are growing strong bones. Your vet will recommend what is best for your puppy. If your puppy or dog gets too fat, you are going to have to put them on a diet just like people should do when they get too fat!

8. It's time to go potty!

Most puppies need to go potty after they eat, drink and play a lot. Puppies pee a lot! You need to keep your eyes on them and use your instincts to recognize when your puppy needs to "go out". They usually need to "go out" every two hours. You will be able to tell when your puppy wants "to go out" because he will start sniffing around anxiously trying to find a good place to pee! Time to whoosh them outside on their leash! If you don't want your pup pooping all over the yard as an adult, pick one area and take him directly there when it's potty time.

9. It's time to play!

Once you have fed your puppy and taken him out to go potty, it is time to let your puppy play. Let him walk, run, and explore outdoors in a confined and safe area at least twice a day. Depending on your puppy's breed and size, most average puppies need a good 20 to 30 minutes of play time. Puppies learn about their surroundings, other animals, and people by sniffing! Sniffing is their roadmap to the world!

JUST LIKE YOU GET THIRSTY, SO DOES YOUR PUPPY!

10. It's time to Teach Your Puppy!

Puppies can be taught the commands 'sit,' 'down,' and 'stay' using a method called food-lure training." Offer you puppy small amounts of food to get him to understand that when he obeys the words, he will get rewarded with a treat. You can also use training treats for puppies instead of food. Over time, the phrase good boy/good girl/ good dog and the affectionate pat and belly rub become secondary reinforcers and you won't need to use the food lure anymore!

It is important to train your puppy with only one command at a time. If you try to teach him too many commands all in one day, he won't remember, he will be confused and he will not learn well. Once your puppy responds to you and you know he understands the command and performs it, you can move to another command. Each time you train your puppy, revisit the commands he already has learned.

If he needs a refresher course, do that before going on to another command.

- **Sit.** The sit command means the dog's hips are on the ground while the shoulders are upright. Reward with treat once she sits down.

- **Come.** The come command in dog training means stop what you're doing, ignore distractions, and go directly to you. Reward with treat once she comes to you. Use puppy's name frequently when training this command.

- **Down.** …Means stop jumping on you or furniture or guests. Say it firmly. Turnaway from your puppy when he jumps on you. Reward with a Good Boy! And a pat on his head. If your puppy keeps jumping, teach him that he will receive no attention for jumping on you or anyone else.

You can turn your back and only pet your dog when all four paws are on the floor. Teach your **dog to do something that is incompatible with jumping up**, such as sitting. They can't sit and jump up at the same time.

- **Stay**. Put your hand out to the puppy and say "Stay". Move backward a little bit at a time and each time put your hand out and say "Stay". When your puppy stays when you move, immediately say "Good Boy/Girl" and reward with a training treat.

- **Outside**. When your puppy has eaten or drank a lot of water, he will probably have to go out. Stand by the door to go out and say, "Do you want to go out?" Your puppy will learn quickly what that means. You should get his leash on quick as you can. When he indicates he wants to go out, always take him!

- **Go to bed.** Show your puppy her bed. Say "Go to bed" by pointing your hand toward her bed or kennel. If you aren't going to bed at the same time, you will probably have to close the kennel door or your bedroom door if your puppy sleeps on a dog bed.

- **Dinner. "Are You Hungry?"** Let the puppy see you get is food bowl out and ready to make his dinner. Let him smell the food before you put it down on the floor and ask him "Are you Hungry"? Tell him he's a good dog as you put his food down and then walk away. Dogs really don't like people or other pets hanging around them while they eat. Make sure his water bowl is filled with fresh water and put it down next to his food bowl. Dogs love to eat! This is an easy task for them!

- **Go for a walk?** It's time to go for a walk. Pick up the collar and leash and ask this question. Puppy will quickly learn what this means.

- **Go Get it!** When you are playing with your puppy, this is a good time to show him his ball or toy and throw it out and tell him to "go get it!" Say it with enthusiasm so your puppy is excited to get it for you.

- **Bring it here.** At the same time, tell your puppy to bring it back when he gets it and reward him with a treat until he just naturally wants to play fetch with you!

- **Drop it!** When you want your puppy to spit out what's in his mouth, firmly say "drop it!". Hold the treat in your hand so he can see and smell it and only give it to him when he drops what's in his mouth. If the treat isn't enough, a peanut butter treat or a piece of cheese will surely entice him to drop whatever he has in his mouth.

11. It's Time for Bed

It is going to be a long night! Puppies get lonely and scared! They will whimper and cry. You won't get much sleep, and neither will he. During the first 2 or 3 weeks, let your puppy sleep next to your bed in his own bed or crate. Make his crate comfy with blankets and cuddly soft toy. When he cries, and he will, it is best to put his leash on and let him pee outside if possible or on a pee pad. Then back to bed with no playing or cuddling. He needs to learn it is "time to go to sleep". Tell him that each night when it is time for bed. Be consistent. And unless you want to have a lifelong bedmate with your puppy, don't take him to bed with you!

12. It's Time to Groom your Puppy

There are a lot of different opinions about grooming puppies and dogs. We are going to keep it simple! Your puppy will probably not need to be groomed until she is 10 to12 weeks old. But, if your puppy plays outside a lot in dirt or mud or dirty water, she might need to be bathed sooner. Try not to bathe a puppy before she is 8 weeks old. First fill up the bathtub or the sink you are going to bathe your puppy in with warm water. Not too hot or not too cold. She won't like it.

Put your puppy gently into the bath.

Let her wiggle around but don't let her jump up.

Once she is relaxed, put some puppy shampoo in your hand and gently massage onto puppy's hair.

Use a very soft, clean washcloth to very gently clean around your puppies.

Wipe out her ears gently with the clean, soft washcloth. Dogs ears are very sensitive and it is best to have a professional clean out her ears.

Take your puppy gently out of the bath and dry her with the towel. Do the best you can.Dogs always "shake" water off their bodies after a bath. So take them to a safe place to dry them and let them shake it off!

If your puppy has a lot of furry hair around her face and ears, don't trim it when she is wet. Only trim it when she is dry.

You can use a dog nail cutter, but we recommend for nail trimming, take your puppy to a groomer or your vet. It is easy to hurt your puppy if you don't cut her nails correctly.

13. Enjoy Your Puppy!

Your successful training is a testament to your love for your puppy and his love for you. He has learned to trust you and will do everything he can to make you proud of him! Remember, training your puppy takes time. You will have the best results by remaining consistent throughout his life with teaching him lessons you want him to learn!

Always praise your puppy by name when he is good. Pat his head and tell him out loud what a good dog he is being. Never yell at or hit your puppy when he is bad. You don't want to punish your puppy. Be positive and reinforce the behavior you want to see from him so he doesn't get confused.

In the end, you want a dog who obeys you and listens to you because he loves you, not because he is afraid of you.

14. Warnings!

NEVER leave your puppy or your dog outside when it is freezing out.

NEVER leave your puppy or dog outside when it is very hot.

NEVER leave your pets in a parked car with windows closed, especially in hot weather. Car interiors heat up to such high temperatures, it can unhappily kill your pet and everyone will be very sad.

Remember, DOGS DON'T SWEAT. If it's too hot for you, it is even hotter for you puppy! The only way you can keep them from overheating and becoming very sick is to keep them cool with lots of water. A b

15. About the Author

Joan lives in Colorado with her husband, two dogs, and a bevy of grandchildren always in and out! Her two dogs consist of a 10 year old puggle and a 2 year old black mouth cur. Both were adopted. Joan has raised and rescued a long line of puppies and breeds for over 45 years. Frequently you will find her home with up to 4 or 5 dogs she has adopted and trained! All her pets lived out long, healthy and happy lives, some for over 20 years! This is a testament for her simple and successful ways to train puppies and older dogs alike! She learned from her dad how to properly care for and train puppies because he raised Labrador retrievers! Joan has published creative and nonfictional essays and stories throughout her college careers and now has turned back to that passion in her sterling age!

16. RESOURCES

American Kennel Club.org

VCA Hospitals.com

The Puppy Academy.com

IAABC Foundation iaabc.org

whole-dog-journal.com/

tractive.com

ASPCA.org

AVSAB.org American Veterinary Society

Positively.com

Made in the USA
Monee, IL
11 December 2022

21058984R00044